Shoulda, Woulda, Coulda

Pam Willis-Hovey

and

Elaine Johnson

Shoulda, Woulda, Coulda

Pam Willis-Hovey

and
Elaine Johnson

Cover Photo Credit

Shawn Woodley

Ghostwritten by Elaine Johnson

CHER⊕KEE PRESS

3425 Cherokee Ave.
Columbus, GA 31906
706-323-2759

DEDICATION

In memory of my mother-in-law
Carol Hovey
who taught me not to live a Shoulda, Woulda, Coulda life
with thanks to all who made this book possible.

Contents

SHOULDA, WOULDA, COULDA

Chapter 1: The Meeting

The bell on the door tinkled and a draft of cold air gusted in the brightly lit room. Johanna glanced up from her textbook, then looked around. Where was Pedro?

The customer shook the rain off his shoulders, then stepped into the room. He slammed the door shut, rattling the sign, "Philly's Best Men's Clothing." Pedro was mysteriously silent; he must have stepped out for a break. She slid her calculations surreptitiously under the counter, and waited one more minute for Pedro. He was always complaining that she took all the customers, but if he wasn't here, well then, she really needed another commission. She glanced around, shrugged, and turned to the customer. Her mouth slightly dropped open. She blinked, then closed her mouth, shook her head, straightened, smoothed her tight black skirt, and stepped smoothly from the counter.

"May I help you?"

"Yes, please. I'm here for the Oil Refiners Convention and the airline lost my luggage. There's a dinner tonight. I need a suit."

She assessed him with a quick, practiced eye. 6' 5". Maybe 250 pounds. In great shape. High-end, quality jacket. Nice shoes. Was that a Rolex?

"We can certainly help. What were you looking for?"

"It has to be a charcoal gray, tailored suit with a short jacket. Oh, and it must be a pinstripe."

"I see. Sir, will you be wearing cuff links?"

He nodded, "Of course."

Johanna fumbled for a tape measure. "We always check the sizes of our clients. May I?"

"Of course, Miss....?"

Why was she blushing? She never blushed. "Johanna."

"It's nice to meet you, Miss Johanna. I'm Jeremiah."

He had a baritone timbre in his voice. His eyes crinkled as he smiled. He had dark, chocolate eyes, but his irises seemed to have a hint of, was it gold? He shook off his jacket and stepped to the three-way mirror. She glanced from his rippling pecs to his tight abs, then to his seat and tripped into the counter. She gulped, then looked down. Her hands were empty. What could have happened to the tape measure? She knelt in her high heels, then grabbed the tape measure from the floor. She rose, breathless, her eyes roving from his rock hard chin to the muscles showing in his neck. "Get a grip," she told herself and took a deep breath. Then, she smiled professionally and moved into action.

At the end, she frowned slightly, tapping her fingers. Most of the clients didn't have such a perfect body. He needed a suit for tonight. What did they have in stock that didn't need much alteration?

The bell on the door tinkled again and a small, older man came through, sneezing.

Still pondering, she called out, "One minute, sir."

Pedro materialized as though waiting for that exact moment. Her forehead wrinkled. Where had he been?

Pedro moved swiftly to the customer, murmured briefly, and the customer left. Pedro came over to her and murmured, "Perhaps the suit in the back?"

Jeremiah was looking worried. "Miss, my convention is starting within a few hours."

She frowned, then followed Pedro. Behind the dark closet, Pedro whipped out a Canali.

"Where did that come from?"

"Oh, uh, it's a return."

"But I don't understand, how did we get a return in the exact size?"

"Hmmm. That is a coincidence."

She shrugged, "Sam, are you busy? Oh, there you are. We're going to have a rush alteration."

Sam moaned. She smiled brightly, held the suit up high, pivoted, and came back in. "We have just the thing for you."

Jeremiah grinned, revealing a slight dimple on his right cheek. Her stomach lurched. She gulped, then stuttered, "Why don't you try it on?"

She stared straight into space after he disappeared with the suit for a long moment, then began hastily assembling ties, and thinking that maybe the Dion shirt would be better with his salt and pepper hair. There was also the Perry Ellis, but no, it was just the least bit too casual. He needed something with a little more flair for his mahogany skin.

Her eyes narrowed as Jeremiah came out of the dressing room.

"It's a winner."

She breathed a sigh.

Sam appeared and began marking the suit. "It only needs a few tucks."

She nodded, waiting politely as the tailor tapped the shoulder pads. The customer already fit the suit better than most. In the mirror, her eyes moved from his broad shoulders to his solid torso. She stared into the depths of his eyes as the tailor bent down, grunting his usual, "Don't move now."

She studied the little dimple on his cheek.

Sam broke her trance, "There, that should do it. Give me a couple of hours."

She nodded beatifically as Jeremiah went back to the dressing room. With his mesmerizing eyes gone, her brain began to function again. Then it hit her. A $1,400.00 sale. The commission would be....The calculations cleared her mind instantly.

When he came out of the dressing room, she smiled at his perfect teeth, then pressed forward with her suggestions of shirts and ties.

And then he needed cufflinks, of course.

And really, his shoes weren't going to work.

The sale eventually ran into the suit (high-end quality with rush alterations), shoes, socks, two shirts, three ties, a belt, and cufflinks.

Pedro came out, but he wasn't whistling as he dealt with the steady inflow of customers, most of whom seemed to want socks.

At the end, she was starting to feel the high of the rush. Jeremiah asked if he could give a tip, and she smiled. "Of course." His aftershave wafted gently in the air as he shifted for the pen.

It was a big tip. She ran the credit card. He smiled looking deeply into her eyes, then checked his watch and swore briefly. "Gotta run."

"Well, sir, enjoy your stay here in Philly and come back again."

Johanna bit her lip, horrified that she wanted to ask when she'd see him again. She smiled brightly as he exited. She sniffed the last whiff of aftershave, hearing him call, "Taxi!" There was a squeal of brakes, then he disappeared with a car door slam.

She turned back. The commission on this one sale would

take care of the rest of the rent! The colors in the room seemed vibrant and new.

The bell on the door tinkled again and she looked up expectantly. An old woman came up, "Miss, can you tell me where the men's underwear is?"

"Over there on the wall."

"Could you get me a size medium? I'm just too tired to find one more thing."

She smiled through her teeth, went over and trudged back with the white underwear, sized medium, worrying about when she'd study for her exam tonight.

…

Two weeks later, Pedro stood outside in the back, keeping a careful two feet from Mr. Paul's fender, "Hey man, you're welcome, but you know, if the boss found out, I'd be in big trouble."

Mr. Paul leaned back on his car and folded his arms, "Come on. I've never seen anyone with a better eye for clothes. She always makes me look good. He really needed the right touch. And who knows, they might hit it off together."

It took Pedro a moment to realize that he wasn't joking, "Johanna doesn't need anyone. She just left her boyfriend. A girl like that, with those curves. She can get anyone she wants. And she's smart. She's going to school. She's studying Business Administration or something like that. She's got looks and brains. She can find her own men."

Mr. Paul straightened up, "Come on. Jeremiah's my friend. He's been through a hard time. I knew the first time I saw her that she was for him. He needs someone special. And it's just a sale. Who knows what happens after that? I don't want him looking bad. He needs to look good. He represents my agency."

Pedro looked down and kicked the ground.

Mr. Paul reached into his back pocket, "Would another $100 make you willing to set it up?"

Pedro laughed, "You know I was risking my job to throw that sale. And I lost money on it too. I didn't think he'd buy much, but the commission on that sale, it should have been mine. I'd have been just as well off taking the commission as the $100 you paid me for setting them up. Sorry man, if he comes back in here, I'm not setting it up."

Mr. Paul flipped through his wallet, "$200 to set them up again. They just need a little push, and I need this guy to come back to Philly to seal this deal."

Pedro shook his head, "I don't know. Johanna is my friend and I don't know anything about this Jeremiah. It was one thing that one time, but doing it again, I'm not so sure."

After a long moment, Mr. Paul showed him a handful of crisp, new bills, "My brother's name is Jeremiah. He is a well-known oil refiner and business owner in Texas. You can check him out online. Just type in 'Jeremiah oil business owner'. That is all you need to know. Once you check him out for yourself, call me. Here is my name and number."

Pedro's eyes widened. He hesitated, and Mr. Paul started to put the bills away. "Wait." Pedro squinted, then pulled out his cell phone and tapped a few times. He glanced up, then tapped some more. After a moment, he whistled.

Paul fingered $50 bills, counted them off, then handed them over, "Please don't tell Johanna that Jeremiah is requesting her presence."

Pedro hesitated, took them, and stuffed them in his pocket as he went back inside.

Paul's phone began to hum. As he opened his car door, he punched a button, "Jeremiah. Hey, my man. I was just talking about you."

The phone was a little crackly. Paul inserted the key in the ignition. "Jeremiah, I've got it covered. Once you get into town I will have all your information on the lady."

Paul shifted the phone, "Jeremiah, I know you want to know right now!" Paul laughed, easing into the tight space between cars. "Sorry, my friend. You will have to wait."

Well, in three weeks Jeremiah had to come to Philly for a meeting, so Paul arranged for a car to pick him up and bring them to their office. At the meeting, Paul started off slowly, "Jeremiah, let's get lunch before we discuss business."

They went to their usual five-star restaurant on the river that always had great lobster. Jeremiah loves sun tea while discussing big matters.

After an eternity of arguing about the proposed oil rig purchases, Paul said, "Jeremiah are you ready to hear about the lady?"

Jeremiah froze.

"Her name is Johanna. She is 21 years old and a college student. She's struggling a little. From what they say at her place of work she is a good, hard worker and smart."

Jeremiah stayed tense. "Any relationships?"

Paul shrugged, "Apparently she's just out of a bad one. It lasted a few years."

Jeremiah gritted his teeth. "She's just out of it? She'll probably want to go back. Go figure." He shook his head, "A woman like that wouldn't just be available."

Paul held up a hand, "I don't think so. Not this time. From what I hear, she would come to work with bruises and marks. She's got a court order for him to stay away."

Jeremiah relaxed, "How long ago?"

Paul shook his head, "This was a couple of months ago. She's pretty busy with school, but apparently there are lots of guys after her. You'd better make a move fast."

Jeremiah nodded, "Paul, you are my boy! I feel the need to buy another suit while I am in town!"

Chapter 2: Encounter

Johanna looked around the empty store. She tapped her fingers on the perfectly clean counter and studied the neatly stacked shirts. She traced a finger along the rigid line of suits. She moved one shoe slightly to the right, frowned, then stepped back. After a moment, she moved it back, sighed, and went back to the cash register. A clock ticked on the wall.

Her cell phone rang. She glanced around the room again, then fumbled with the phone. "Hello."

She groaned and looked around furtively. No one was within earshot, but she turned her back anyway.

"Yes, this is Johanna."

"Well, yes. I am aware that my rent is a little past due, but well, school is really expensive."

The clock ticked louder.

"No, no. Well, yes, I do get a grant, but it doesn't cover half of my expenses."

"Yes, I know, but I'm on commission and it's been slow this month. I mean, I don't have any money."

She nodded at the phone, then sighed. It was time to tell the truth, "What happened was this. My mama had to have an operation. The medical bills have been really high. If you can just give us some time, we'll get back on our feet soon."

Her eyes widened.

"Eviction! Oh please don't do that! Eviction! Where will we go? Can't you do something? Anything? There's got to be a way out of this."

"Another two days? That's all? Well, I'll see what I can do. Two days. Yes, yes. Of course, I agree it's nice of you. Two days."

The door opened and the bell tinkled. "I have to go. Yes, Two days. Got it."

She moved out to the customer, but he turned and left the store. Her shoulders drooped.

The store phone rang, and she heard Pedro pick up. She pressed her fingers against her temples, trying to massage away the pounding, when Pedro tapped her and handed her the store phone.

"Johanna, it's me, Paul, your favorite longtime customer."

She shifted as Pedro moved behind her, heading back to the offices. "Oh hi, Mr. Paul, how are you?"

"I'm fine, Johanna. How long are you working tonight?"

"The store closes at 8, but I'm supposed to be off now." She stopped herself, "I'll be here till 8."

"Great, I have a friend that has come in town. We are in need of a tailored suit."

"Certainly, sir. I will be happy to wait on you!"

"We're on our way."

Johanna hung up the phone, went on wobbly legs in the restroom, and stood behind the door. In her heart, she screamed, "Thank You, God!"

Fifteen minutes later, she saw the picture of professionalism as two tall, mahogany men walked in the store.

Johanna said, "Well! Hello again, sir."

Jeremiah replied, "How are you doing, young lady?"

She smiled, "Sir, I am great now!"

Jeremiah had a puzzled look on his face, confused by her answer.

She tried to cover it up, "I always wondered how everything went with your convention. Did the airlines ever return your suit?"

He nodded, "The convention was good but it could have been better. To answer your second question: no, they never found my suit, but they replaced its value."

Paul interjected, "Jeremiah, I have an appointment. I need to leave."

Jeremiah started, "Now?"

Paul began moving out, "Yes, I forgot to tell you that I set up a late dinner with one of our clients and this was the only time I could meet with them." In the long silence, Paul went on, "Man, you know how business goes. If you want that sale, then you will meet with the client whatever time that they say."

Jeremiah looked puzzled, "Ok." After a moment, he went on. "Partner, who is this? You never said anything about it up to now."

Paul nodded, "I know. I wanted to surprise you with the details once I got everything finalized. Go ahead and don't keep Johanna waiting."

Jeremiah held up his hand, "Paul, don't forget we rode here together, man. I guess I have to get a ride?"

Paul shook his head, "Now you know I would not leave you like that. Johanna, would you like to make double commission and a big tip tonight?"

She looked up with big eyes, "Mr. Paul, are you asking me for help?"

"Yes, can you take my friend to the house up on the golf course? I will have the car place that I own send a car for him. If you would, go with him to ensure he's at the right place and then bring my purchases to my office." He was moving fast, but turned at the door, "Come by my office. I will have a check to cover your expenses for tonight."

"Thank you, sir. I will take care of Jeremiah for you. No worries."

"Jeremiah, is that ok with you?"

Jeremiah looked sideways at Johanna. "Well Johanna, I am yours for the evening. Let's get this sale on the way! Johanna, as we look, tell me a little bit about yourself."

Neither heard the door click. "Right now I am in school full time. I work part time here, selling men's suits. Sir, school is kicking my behind real bad."

She pulled out a dark gray shirt and held it up to his face, then shook her head and put it back. Jeremiah asked, "Why?"

"This semester includes Advanced Accounting and math has always been my struggle. It kills me." She chose a lighter gray, and held it up, then stood back, undecided.

Jeremiah was thinking, "Johanna, can your parents help with a tutor?"

"No sir, right now they are both on Social Security."

His voice softened, "Johanna, if you don't mind, why are they on SSI?"

She put the gray back, studied the row and then pulled a light blue one. "My parents both have health issues which forced them to retire early. My father is a good man and a deacon in the church and my mother sings in the choir." She put the blue next to his face and stepped back. "Jeremiah, before they got sick they were cooks at the college I attend. I have one sister named Lydia. She is a secretary at a law firm here. My sister and I live together." She nodded and moved the shirt a little higher. "I think this color works well on you."

"Wow. Johanna you have a remarkable story. It sounds like you've worked hard."

"Oh yes, we work for what's ours. Someday I hope to own a suit store. Jeremiah, I will say this. I am already saving up for it." The shirt, forgotten, was on the counter. Her back was to the clothing. "May I ask how old you are?"

"I am 21 years old working on my second year of college. Once I finished high school I took a year off to have fun and save some money working full time."

Her mind came back to reality. "Ok, Jeremiah let me show you a suit. To be honest, I am enjoying your company." Johanna was blushing while he stared into her eyes. "Well sir, tell me about you?"

He followed her to the suit racks, "About me. I have my oil refinery. I am here visiting my friend Paul for business. We are long-time friends and fraternity brothers. Johanna, we go way back to high school days. We played football together." He shook his head at her first choice, "I don't think that color works as well in Texas." She nodded, put it back, then moved her fingers along the row before selecting another one, "We hoped to make the NFL back then, but that did not happen. We both come from famous families that you would know. His family is known for making cakes and pies. They've had a national franchise for something like 30 years. After Paul left college, he worked the family business and turned it into a multi-million dollar enterprise."

His eyes were distant remembering. He came back with a shrug, "My family owned real state. One of our properties had oil on it. We hit it over 30 years ago and I too, like

21

Paul, worked the family business. Johanna, from that start, I revamped about 12 years ago. It's big on the gulf, in Texas, and overseas."

Johanna stared, her mouth open, the jacket almost dragging the floor. "May I ask how old you are now?"

He laughed ruefully, "I am 41 years old."

"Wow!"

He turned his back on the suits, "I hope that's good?"

"Yes sir, you don't look it."

"Johanna, you speak my kind of language. Johanna, I must say I admire a hard-working woman. To be so young, you've got a head on you. Of course, you are so beautiful."

"Now Jeremiah, I am flattered. When you are a big girl like a size 18, you don't hear that much."

"Johanna, I liked what I saw the first time I saw you." He shifted awkwardly. After a long moment, he went on, "I hope that my age does not stop you from wanting to get to know me?"

"Well Jeremiah, I can say the same, can't I? To be honest I am feeling a little uncomfortable about this conversation. Jeremiah, can I sell you a suit or what?"

"Johanna what does, 'or what' mean?"

The pounding in her temples was gone! When did that happen? "Would you rather get a bite to eat and do the sale tomorrow? Because right now I only have 30 minutes until the store closes."

He glanced at his watch, "Let's go out and I will shop with you tomorrow."

"Ok, well, wait in the lobby because I have to close my register out." Everything was fine with my lady. Johanna walked away from him switching those hips in her high heels. Jeremiah stared at all that too! As she was counting down her draw, she felt disbelief. Why would this millionaire want to get to know her? She looked down at her Payless shoes.

Sana came up next to her. "I heard all that."

"Oh?"

"What is Mr. Paul up too?" She was shaking her head. "It is no accident that Mr. Paul forgot to make arrangements for his friend to get home. These two are up to something. Driving Jeremiah from downtown Philly up to Mr. Paul's house is what? An hour?"

Johanna lost her count and put the coins back in the drawer. "No, it's more like a 30-minute ride one way. I know because I've gone with Pedro sometimes to fit him for suits."

Sana's eyes narrowed. "This is your chance. If you can pull a man like this, your financial worries will be over."

Johanna shook her head nonchalantly. "Maybe. That's not what I'm looking for."
Sana was urgent, "Listen to me. This man can fast-track

your life. Maybe like everything else in your life, it's a shoulda, woulda, coulda. You told me yourself just last night. Every time you think you have the perfect man, then for some reason or another, it falls apart."

Johanna shrugged. She carefully put some numbers on the form and zipped the bag.

Sana looked around, "Look, I remember you coming in with bruises every day. I see you working all the time and spending all your free time studying. This is your chance. Take it." She hugged her hard, and then started off but turned at the door, "Throw caution to the wind."

Johanna looked a long time in the mirror, then moved to the employee's lockers.

. . .

Jeremiah was out front, on the phone, pacing. "She is intelligent, sexy, and beautiful. All that. More. Yes, more."

He walked around, looked up, put one hand on his hip, and swiveled. "Well, there is one issue going on in my head. I am 41. Next thing is, well, I have been legally separated for over a year. Will she still go out with me if I tell her?"

He nodded his head a few times, then held the phone away and shook his head in disgust, "What do you mean, what's the issue? I'm telling you, she's not that kind of a woman."

"It's like this," He took a deep breath and then blew it out, "Most women that come from a Christian background won't go out with a man that is still married, even if he is going through a divorce."

"Well, I wanted you to know that I'm taking her to dinner."

Paul's voice could be heard clearly through the phone, "Man, did you buy a suit?"

Jeremiah began pacing again, "No, we decided to get a bite to eat and converse with each other more."

Paul said, "Well?"

"Well, what?"

"Man, you know?"

"Paul, she is nice and has a hard time in college, that's all. She comes from humble beginnings."

The voice on the phone was a little garbled. Jeremiah moved to the right a little and shifted his head down a bit. Paul's voice came in, "Jeremiah, I know you've got a weakness for women. But this time, please take your time. This one is half your age."

"Paul, I hear you but this young lady is different. Call me crazy but I feel good about her."

"Yes, Jeremiah, but you said that about the other women before her." The crackle in the phone was getting louder. "As your bro, I've got your back. Has the driver came with the Bentley? No? Hang up. I will call you."
Jeremiah finally stopped pacing and waited. Pedro came

out, "Sir? Sir, a driver has called to say he will be here in 15 minutes. He is en route."

Jeremiah was checking email. Pedro moved forward, "Johanna says she will be with you shortly."

Jeremiah smiled and said thank you, typing an answer. Pedro came closer, "Are you THE Jeremiah? The one with the big refinery out of Texas that was featured in Time magazine?"

Jeremiah pressed send, then put the phone away, "Yes."

Pedro was stuttering, "Wow, it's a pleasure to meet you, sir. You are the talk of social media and MSNBC. I can't believe you are here in our store."

Jeremiah smiled, "Yes, my friend Paul shops here a lot and told me to come here back when the airline lost my prized suit."

Pedro nodded, "Paul requested that Johanna take care of you."

Jeremiah had pretty much figured that out, "That is good to know."

"Well sir, she's our top sales agent."

Johanna walked out in her silk wrap dress. It was a mid-length dress with a V neck and split on the side. That blue shade always made her feel beautiful and so did her glittering high heeled sandals. She had a short-cut afro with a silver tint. She comes from a line of women in her family that gray early. Jeremiah began smiling away.

Just then, the car pulled up. The driver got out and came up, "Hi, Mr. Jeremiah. I am your driver. Mr. Paul told me to take care of you." Then he spoke to Johanna, "How are you?"

"I am fine, sir."

The driver opened the door, "So where are we headed? Mr. Paul said I am to take you wherever you want to go."

Jeremiah hesitated, then looked at Johanna. It had been a long time since lunch, "I am ready to eat."

The driver said, "There is a nice restaurant around the corner that serves great Italian food and they have live music."

It was the easiest decision Jeremiah made that day, "Ok! Let's go."

Chapter 3: Falling

As she scooted into the Bentley, Johanna muttered to herself, "Keep it together, keep it together, act cool." She gracefully settled into the cushion, tucking her dress under her thighs like her mother taught her. She settled a little more as the cushions enfolded her and the door quietly shut beside her. Wow. Jeremiah got in on the far side, and after a pause for traffic, so did the driver. Her eyes moved across the gleaming metal, past the tinted glass, and across the dark seat in front. She stroked the leather beside her. Wow. The car smelled of leather and polish and cigars. Everything was dark and shiny and spotless. She was focused on the front, wondering what was in the box, and suddenly realized that the car had pulled out. This was the smoothest ride she'd ever been in. It moved into traffic, then stopped at a light.

Her brain moved into gear, "Don't stare, keep it cool." She pulled her eyes from the box and glanced out the window. The driver in the next car was peering intently into hers, trying to see if anyone famous was in the car. A teenager in the backseat was pointing at the Bentley. She blinked, then looked away. Three kids at the corner were balancing with their skateboards in their hands, ogling the Bentley.

The phone in her purse started vibrating.

She blushed, the light changed and the Bentley moved forward. She half-turned in the seat to see Jeremiah eyeing her, "You're pretty quiet."

Her phone vibrated again. She bit her lips, then smiled at

him. "Would you excuse me?"

She dug into her purse, and internally groaned at the name. She pulled it to her ear. "Lydia, yes, I know. I'm sorry I didn't call. I forgot. I know. You know I always turn the sound off at work. I'm sorry you've been waiting. Listen, sis, I've, um, I've gotten another ride, so just go on home. I'll see you there later. Yes, I know. OK. See you."

The car made a slow right turn as she looked into Jeremiah's upraised eyebrow, "My sister. Sir, we only have one car and she works at a law firm down the street from me. She takes me to school on her lunch break and drops me off at work."

Jeremiah said, "I see."

She couldn't think what to say after that. She clicked the phone and dropped it in her purse. After a long moment, Jeremiah went on, "Johanna, you've got me wondering?"

"Oh? Why?"

He shifted a little, "You said you felt uncomfortable when we were talking at the suit store, but yet you still came out to dinner."

The car slowed down. A delivery person on a motor scooter pulled up next to them and gawked into the windows. His gaze slid past Johanna and he bent down a little to try and get a glimpse of Jeremiah.

She smoothed her dress, "Jeremiah, you know how people are these days. You don't want people thinking that I am trying to get a favor to make a big commission. I just don't need that kind of gossip out. Jeremiah, when I am at work that's what I do: just work."

After a moment, he smiled, "Johanna you are one straightforward woman and I like that."

Out the window, she saw two men yelling. She could see their mouths move, but nothing penetrated the car's cocoon of silence. The Bentley swept past them past and Johanna turned her gaze, "Well Jeremiah, you read me really well."

The car purred to a stop, "Mr. Jeremiah and Miss Johanna, we have arrived at the restaurant." The driver opened the door and Johanna stepped out of the sleek auto.

A few women were standing at the door, whispering and watching. Jeremiah came up to her side and the women bent into each other. Johanna heard, "Time Magazine," and, "Are you sure?", but couldn't catch the rest as she moved past them into the restaurant.

The restaurant had a high ceiling, dark tapestries and gold touches. Lights glowed through the bay windows. Jeremiah moved over to the greeters' table. "We don't have reservations, but hope you can seat us anyway. The name is Jeremiah."

The maître d' nodded, recognizing Jeremiah instantly, then glanced beyond Jeremiah, flicking his eyes up and down over Johanna. "Certainly, sir." He pulled two menus, "This way, please."

Jeremiah motioned for Johanna to go first, and she stepped out, her high heels clicking on the hardwood floors, into the dark room lit with slanting candles and muted lighting. Her dress swishing against her legs, she moved down a long aisle, past the murmurs of diners, the clink of silverware, and the tablecloths gently swaying. A band on the far wall played soft jazz with the spotlight dim on the singer.

The maître d' came to a booth at a window. Johanna slipped in and the cushion sank as Jeremiah moved on to his side. She took the menu with a murmured, "Thank you."

"Your server will be with you shortly."

Jeremiah nodded, but Johanna was too entranced with the view to notice. Lights glowed on the dark river, winding into the distance. Trees blotted most of the view, but the reflections on the river shone. Was that a boat in the back? She looked up to see Jeremiah gazing intently at her face. The band swung into a different tune and there was a smattering of laughter at the next table. The candle at their table cast a deep shadow across his face, but picked up a gold tone in his irises.

"This is a wonderful view."

Jeremiah tore his eyes away, glanced outside and then back. "Yes, it is."

The music stopped. There was a short shuffle, then it started again, with a slower tune, a saxophone picking up the melody.

The candle at her table flickered.

She felt a motion to her left, then a man, clothed in black, came to the table, picked up a glass, and began to pour water. "Good evening," He had some sort of accent. She'd heard it before, "I'll be your server tonight."

He stopped, "Johanna?"

Johanna twisted in her seat, "Caesar, I didn't know you worked here!"

She looked up to a tall, muscular, soccer player with dark, intent eyes. Even the dim lighting, Caesar looked better, if that was possible, in the restaurant than he did in History 220.

At 21 years old, 5 feet and 10 inches, and 175 lbs., he was the first Italian she'd ever known. He had that nice olive skin and that long, black Italian hair that was now tied back, but usually spilled over his broad shoulders. Caesar and Johanna had been friends since her freshman year of college, when Caesar introduced himself. He told her that he had just arrived from Rome and hadn't met any Americans. He mused that he loved her personality and her hazel green eyes. She didn't really know what to make of that, but eventually chalked it up to him being a foreigner. After all, he did lots of things that were really different. Maybe he just meant it to be friendly, not understanding the language and all.

Every time she looked at him, Johanna felt something a whole lot more than friendliness. She wanted to tell Caesar how she felt, but fear set in every time she opened her mouth. Once she saw him on her street, which made her start thinking Caesar might be looking for her. Maybe he wanted to be more than friends, but the next time she saw him, he ducked his head, so she wasn't so sure. He said the strangest things and he seemed really shy sometimes. They never dated because the one time he stopped by the house, her mother was there. Mama got very quiet as he was introduced. After he left, Mama started talking about girls who went outside their race. Caesar worked out and was in great shape; she wasn't sure how he felt about her weight. Johanna fidgeted slightly with her dress, then looked up to see both men staring at her cleavage.

"Jeremiah, this is Caesar. He's studying at my university."

Jeremiah sat back, looked up at Caesar, then nodded. Caesar's eyes flicked from Jeremiah to Johanna and then down to her cleavage, then back to Jeremiah. He frowned. "It's good to meet you, sir." His eyes glared at the two of them, then he seemed to realize where he was. His face went bland and smooth, although his lips were a little pursed.

He set her filled glass down, ignoring the dark stain that spread around it. Johanna couldn't help but ask, "Caesar, when did you start working here?"

"Not that long ago. About 3 weeks." Caesar picked up Jeremiah's glass. "My cousin from Rome has a couple of restaurants here in the US including this one, so he gave me a job. It's the only job I'm allowed to have with my student visa." He turned to Jeremiah, "I'm here on a fellowship," His eyes went back to the glass. He hesitated, then started to fill it a bit more, "but he's family. Pretty, huh!" His eyes swept Jeremiah, then darted back, and he froze. The pitcher kept pouring, "Wait. I recognize you. You were on Time magazine. And TV." He jerked the pitcher as the water overflowed. He fumbled for a cloth, then wiped the glass, and wiped and wiped and wiped. He breathed in and out, then choked out, trying to be nonchalant, "So, Mr. Jeremiah, how are you?"

"Caesar, I'm fine." Jeremiah closed the menu.

Caesar renewed his wiping. His voice was strangled, "Can I ask you a question?"

Jeremiah looked startled, "Sure."

"Mr. Jeremiah, you're one of the most successful oil tycoons of the year." Caesar carefully placed the glass on the crisp, white tablecloth.

"Well, Caesar, that's me."

Caesar jerked the pitcher and a little water sloshed out, "What brings you to Philly? I can't believe you chose my family's business."

"Well, my partner Paul has an oil convention here and that brought me to town. My driver recommended this place. He said it's good."

Caesar leaned forward, his eyes alight. "Sir, I don't want to hold you up, but can I ask one more question?"

Jeremiah tensed, "Yes."

Johanna was starting to wonder if this conversation was ever going to end. She glanced at her watch without anyone noticing. No wonder she was so hungry.

Caesar didn't blink, "We have career day at our college this week. Since you are here in town, would you consider being on the line-up for one day?"

Jeremiah relaxed slightly, "Yes, but let me check with my secretary back home. I will have her contact your college."

"Thanks," Caesar said, "Oh, uh."

A server appeared magically, knelt down and wiped the floor. Caesar backed up, bumped into the next table, turned and shifted from foot to foot, then mumbled something and left.

Johanna hesitated until the server finished cleaning the floor. She apologized to Jeremiah for her friend.

Jeremiah shrugged, "That's fine. I'm used to it." His dark eyes flickered from Caesar's retreating figure, "You know, Johanna, we are looking for college students for an internship to help us promote and market our new motor oil."

"Wow, Jeremiah, that's great. This would be a great opportunity for us students. I can hardly wait!"

He smiled, "So you'll be there. Johanna, like I told your friend, I will check my calendar and see how to make your career day." He reached across the table and brushed her hand. Johanna smiled at Jeremiah and then brushed his thumb. With a surprising strength, his fingers closed on hers.

"Johanna," Jeremiah seemed to be choosing his words carefully, "I don't mind a person talking to me. That comes with being a celebrity. Right now I would rather get to know this lady in front of me." Jeremiah seemed mesmerized by her smile and those green eyes.

Caesar came to the table to take their order. He was a lot quieter this time, and glanced nervously at the door to the kitchen. Jeremiah ordered salmon with basil and Johanna chose cheese ravioli with asparagus. Caesar frowned at their hands, clasped across the table. He took the order, then turned and left.

"Are you into jazz?"

Jeremiah nodded, "They're pretty good." He kept talking, but Johanna's phone vibrated. She kept her face bland, then fumbled in her purse, and glanced down at the number. Oh no. Not here. She hesitated, then shut it off. Jeremiah paused and the music swelled.

Her phone vibrated again, "Could you excuse me?" Jeremiah gestured with his palm, and Johanna slipped away. She went swiftly down the aisle, then stopped. She turned right. The ladies room had to be around here somewhere. She turned walked two steps, then halted. Her phone vibrated again. Lydia would be furious if she didn't answer. Johanna backed against a wall and reached into her purse. A door right around the corner slammed open, making her drop the phone.

She bent down to get it, then glanced through the door and saw into the kitchen. Caesar was across from her. She started to get up, then ducked as he slammed his hand against a wall. His second cousin Vinnie was there too. Vinnie squeezed some herbs into a pot on the stove, "Hey man, what's your problem?"

"Nothing."

Vinnie laughed, "Hey, we were all watching. A Bentley comes to the place; of course, we all stop to see who's in it!"

His other cousin Paulo flipped spaghetti in to a bowl. "Isn't that your girl with him?"

Vinnie tossed the vegetables, "I didn't know you were dating anyone. You got a girl, Caesar?"

As Paulo was trying to select an implement, he said, "Ha, he's not dating anyone. He can't make up his mind, can you Caesar?"

Vinnie turned around, "You're kidding. The girl he's been mooning about? What was her name?" He snapped his fingers, "Johanna. She's here?"

"Shut up," Caesar muttered as he folded bread into a basket.

Paulo pointed a spoon, "You never said she was a looker."

Vinnie laughed, "This is the Johanna that's going to be your date at Augustus' open house! It's the same Johanna, right?"

Paulo, "I don't know. I think it's too late for you Caesar. I think my friend, this Mr. Jeremiah hotshot is putting the moves on your woman!" He pulled the meat off the grill and slapped it on a plate.

Johanna's phone vibrated again, and she scooted to the left, stood and went around the corner before answering. She tried to keep her voice low, "Hey, sis, don't ask questions. I am at a restaurant with Jeremiah, the oil tycoon from Texas."

The screech went up her spine. Johanna pulled the phone away, then shifted the phone to her other ear. She looked around and moved a few steps farther down the wall, and then pressed closer to the wall, "I can't talk right now. I'll tell you all about it later when I get home." She clicked off the protests, moved the phone to silent, took a deep breath and went the other way back to their table, past the band.

Jeremiah stood up as she came closer, "Do you dance?" He held out a hand to her. She smiled, and reached her hand back to his. They swayed back and forth a few times to the beat, then he led her to the dance floor as the band shifted to a faster melody. His arm was firm on her back, and he twirled her lightly, flaring her skirt, before bringing her close for a slow dance.

She started listening to the vocalist. That music, what was it? It was that song from the Cinderella movie. She began singing silently along, "A dream is a wish your heart makes…" She smiled as her blue dress swirled, her feet light on the round wooden floor. Jeremiah guided her gently backwards, then turned her to the left. She smiled up, matching her steps to his. He was so easy to follow.

The song came to an end and they stayed close for a moment, staring into each other's eyes. There was a smattering of chatter nearby. She blinked and the room came back into focus. Jeremiah pressed his arm into her back to nudge her to turn, then took her hand. With his thumb rubbing hers, she moved through the small crowd back to their table, past Caesar, standing at their table serving the food. She slid into the booth.

Caesar scowled as Jeremiah sat down, "Is there anything else?" Jeremiah shook his head. Johanna couldn't think of anything. She didn't notice when Caesar left.

Jeremiah held up a glass. "Bon Appétit!" She clinked her glass with his as the band moved into her favorite song, the candle on their table glowed, and out of the corner of her eye, in the windows, a boat moved slowly up the river. She picked up a fork, glanced up and their eyes locked. She felt like she was drowning.

Johanna tried to break the spell, "Stop! I am trying to eat and you should too. It's been a long day for you."

His fingers moved across the table to twine around hers, "My Lady Johanna, you are so beautiful to me."

She could feel the blush. Her hands trembled. She toyed with his fingers absently, then decided to just say it. "Oh, Jeremiah please forgive for what I am about to say. You are fine." She felt the blush move up her cheeks. "Jeremiah, I hope that is not too forward."

His eyes were soft, "My lady, it's the same for me too."

"Jeremiah, if we don't stop flirting, our food will be cold." Both of them just smiled and laughed at each other.

The time flew by. Jeremiah had one fascinating story after another. He seemed entranced with everything she said. She floated through the meal.

When they finished, Jeremiah took the check. He left three $50.00 bills on the table, then took her hand.

As they walked out, Caesar hurried up, "Sir, you forgot your change."

Jeremiah glanced around, then moved his hand to Johanna's shoulders, and turned away, "Young man, that's for you. Keep up the good work."

Caesar stopped, flustered. As Johanna bent into the Bentley, he called out, "Thanks!"

Moving to the other side of the car, Jeremiah nodded, waved, then bent into the car and pulled out his cell phone as he settled in beside her. She hadn't heard it ring. "Jeremiah here."

The driver was shutting his door and pulling on his seatbelt when Johanna remembered the opening. It was tomorrow. Maybe she should double-check with Caesar and make sure everything was still on?

Jeremiah bent forward, "Can you speak up? There's something wrong with the reception." He shifted the phone higher on his ear and put one hand over the other.

Johanna pushed a button and her window glided silently down. She started to wave, but hesitated when she saw that Vinnie had his hand on Caesar's shoulder. As the Bentley pulled out, she saw Caesar shrug the hand off, and say "Someday, and it's not going to be long, he and I are going to square off about Johanna."

She turned back, flustered. Jeremiah looked at her and

raised an eyebrow.   She shook her head, and he turned back to his call.   The wind was blowing her hair, so she pushed the button.   The dark windows rose as the car hummed down the road.

Chapter 4: It's Working, or Is It?

It only took a few minutes to reach the loft apartment. Once they arrived, Jeremiah hastily hung up, then turned to her, "Johanna, may I call you?"

She sat back in the car, then smiled, "Yes, I wrote my number on the back of my sales associate's card." She hesitated, then thought of Caesar and all the times she wished she'd said something. She swallowed, "Can I have your number as well?"

"My lady, you can have what you want." He pulled out a card, then frowned when he saw her face, "Please don't say you won't go out with me." What should she say to that?

He pressed forward, "Can we go tomorrow?"

She was about to answer when she saw the curtains in her living room shift. Lydia was probably peeking through the curtains, "Jeremiah, I promise I will call you with an answer."

Her door opened, and she climbed out of the Bentley as he came around, "Let me walk you to your door."

What could that hurt? "Ok!"

They strolled, arm in arm, to the door. Jeremiah touched her cheek, "Johanna, may I hug and kiss you?"

Johanna said, "Well, you can hug me but just a kiss on the check for now."

"Alright, my lady Johanna, as you wish."

He engulfed her in his arms, then pushed her back. He stared intently into her eyes, then brushed his lips on her check. "Johanna, good night."

"Same to you, The Jeremiah from Texas." Johanna laughed and smiled.

He smiled also, then stroked her cheek and walked back to the car. He waved from the car, then stood as she found her keys and opened the door.

As soon as Johanna walked inside, Lydia got into it, "Johanna, what is going on? I was waiting and waiting for you when I saw this limo or something pull up. And then my baby sister got out! As you were standing there, I realized. 'Just a minute, this man looks really familiar.' You got closer to the window, and I couldn't believe it. It really was Jeremiah, the multi-million dollar oil tycoon. How in the world did you get with The Jeremiah?"

Johanna turned and locked the door, her fingers lingering on the part of the hand where he touched her. "It's nothing."

"What?"

Her sister pulled open the curtain again, "What kind of car was that you were in?"

Johanna heard the car start up. "Umm. It's a Bentley."

"A Bentley! What were you doing in a Bentley?"

The sound of the car faded away. She looked around at the faded sofa, and the old green recliner, then at the cheap linoleum next to the thin carpet.

Lydia let go of the curtain and turned back, "What's going on?"

Johanna kicked off her shoes and slid her purse off her shoulder, "Mr. Paul buys custom-made suits from our store."

Lydia wasn't expecting a conversation about the store. "I know."

"Well, Jeremiah is his best friend. So he asked me to host his friend while he was tied up in a business meeting. He's going to pay me, and I will pick the check up from his office tomorrow."

Lydia moved back, "Money! Well, thank God for that! You know we are short on the rent."

"I know, sis. This is a blessing for us. I am selling Jeremiah a suit and hosting too."

Lydia threw her hands in the air and began dancing around the living room, "That's amazing!" She stopped, "That's such a relief." She came back to Johanna and hugged her, "I didn't know what we were going to do."

She froze in mid-hug, then pulled back. Lydia looked Johanna up and down frowning, "Johanna, just watch yourself and don't do something that you will feel sorry about." She pulled her close, "Little sis, you know what I mean?"

Johanna hugged her back, "I know. Lydia, we had a great date. Girl, that man's got a bo-flex body and rock hard abs. He works out. Oh, me!" She yawned and stretched, "Lydia, I have had a full day. I'm going to take a shower and go to bed."

Lydia smiled and let her go, "Goodnight, sis. I love you."

...

The next day Johanna called Mr. Paul's office and the secretary answered. "May I help you?"

"Yes, my name is Johanna and I think Mr. Paul has a check for me?"

The secretary hesitated, "Hold on, please, Johanna. Mr. Paul, it's Johanna from the store."

Johanna heard a muffled, "Please put her through." Followed by, "Yes, sir."

Then the phone came in clearly, "Hello, Johanna. How are you?"

"Mr. Paul, I am fine."

"Listen Johanna, I had a call from Mr. Jeremiah. We need to talk about hosting my friend and the check. How soon can you get here?"

She didn't hesitate, "Hold on just a minute." She muted the phone and called out, "Mr. Paul wants me to pick up the check."

Lydia yelled back, "I don't need the car until 5:00 pm. Go ahead."

She unmuted the phone, "Mr. Paul, I will be there in half an hour, sir.

"See you shortly, Johanna."

She skipped out the door, found her sister's car, and shoved the junk on the front seat over, and scooted in. It only took 20 minutes to get downtown.

Mr. Paul was waiting in the lobby for her. "Johanna, we need to talk."

Her stomach quailed, "Mr. Paul, is everything ok?"

"Yes! Johanna, sure. Listen, could you host Jeremiah for the whole weekend? I will pay $500.00 for last night and $1000.00 for the weekend. What do you say?"

She stood speechless. He looked behind her, saw her sister's car, and grimaced. "Don't worry about an automobile because I will arrange for all of that."

Her voice came back, "Why are you doing this for me?"

"Johanna, my friend Jeremiah has been going through something and I have not seen him this happy in a long time." He waited, "Well?"

"Mr. Paul, I want to but I'm supposed to go to an opening in Stone Mountain."

It took him a moment, "You mean, the Stone Mountain in

Georgia?"

She nodded, "They already paid my plane ticket. We are due to leave at 3:00 pm today."

He thought, then looked up, "Johanna, let me see what I can do." He grabbed his a cell phone, then stopped, "Oh, by the way, here is your first check."

He pulled out the check, but hesitated before giving it to her, "Johanna, call me an hour before you get on the plane."

Johanna nodded, "Yes, sir," then floated back to the car and to the apartment.

Lydia was fixing her hair when she came in. Johanna hugged her, then began dancing around the room, "Lydia, Mr. Paul paid me $500.00 to host his friend for yesterday."

Lydia stood staring at the check, "We sure need it for the rent."

Johanna waltzed back, "That's not all! He asked if I'd host Jeremiah for the rest of the weekend - $1,000.00!"

Lydia's mouth dropped. Then she put the check down, "Caesar is our friend and you know that boy likes you, Johanna. You like him, too." She studied Johanna. "Or do you?"

Johanna swept into the middle of the room, "Yes, but Jeremiah is something else and girl, he is too fine!"

Lydia's hand reached to the check. She picked it up,

scrutinized it for a long time, tracing the amount with her trembling finger. She closed her eyes, took a deep breath, then put it face-down on the table, and squared her shoulders, "Johanna, think of the long term! Jeremiah's got deep pockets but Caesar has been there for you." She moved closer to Johanna. "Don't forget when your ex-boyfriend beat you up. Caesar was there for you. I know he has not said how he feels, but he loves you, sis. You haven't said how you feel because of his color."

Johanna stopped in the middle of the floor, "Oh." She began thinking hard about what to do. Her cell phone rang. She glanced at the name and winced. Caesar.

Reluctantly, she pulled the phone to her ear. "Hi, Caesar."

The line had static, "Johanna, are you ready? We have to be at the airport two hours early."

Lydia was glaring at her. Johanna was quiet and slow responding, "Caesar."

The static was worse, "Johanna, what's up?"

She tried to think, "Caesar, I will call you back in an hour."

"What?"

"I can't hear you Caesar, whatever you're saying. Listen, I'll call you back."

"OK."

She put the phone down, and it immediately rang again. Mr. Paul. She looked at Lydia, then put the phone to her ear, "Hi, Mr. Paul."

"Hi Johanna, what is your decision?"

"Mr. Paul, my best friend Caesar has a brother that is a neurosurgeon. His new facility is having an opening in Stone Mountain. This is his day. He paid for us to fly there. I can't let Caesar go alone, I just can't." She swallowed, "Mr. Paul, I will be gone until Monday."

There was a long pause, "Well, Johanna, I have an idea."

"Yes, Mr. Paul."

"My company has a plane. If I fly you to this event, can you return immediately after it's done?"

Johanna blinked a few times, "Let me call you back."

She got off the phone and turned to Lydia who was standing there tapping her foot. The explanation was short, but Lydia just shook her head, "Sis, this is tough. I would love to tell you yes, but Caesar will be hurt. Wow, sis, this Jeremiah guy really likes you. Whatever you do be careful." She studied Johanna carefully, "Johanna, $1,000.00 is a lot of money for the weekend."

Chapter 5: Torn

Johanna hesitated, glanced in the side-view mirror, then pulled into the next lane, pushing the pedal as far to the floor as it would go. The old car hesitated, seemed to gather courage, and picked up speed.

Caesar was busy fiddling with her radio. He pushed another button, shook his head, and then pushed another and another.

He finally got a song going, then settled back in his seat as Johanna slammed on brakes to slow down for the traffic ahead. She studied the side mirror, but it looked like the rest of the lanes weren't moving much better.

Caesar leaned forward to study his mirror, then shook his head and sat back. "It's OK. I've got plenty of time. My flight isn't for another two hours."

The song on the radio came to an end. A plane was low overhead, drowning out the music. After the plane passed, Caesar grimaced at the next tune, and bent towards the radio again. "Say, Johanna."

She braked a bit. "Yes."

"I'm so looking forward to us hanging out in Stone Mountain." He looked up quickly, "But, hey, I understand that you have to work. It's ok." He looked out the window. "Tell me again how this trip is going to work?"

She pulled out into the next lane, as a car honked at her.

"It's great.   Mr. Paul worked it for me to fly back in his plane so I can be in two places at one time."   She pulled over one more lane.

Caesar frowned. The radio was playing static, but neither noticed.

She went on with a rush, "Mr. Paul said that he will refund the purchase cost of the plane ticket to make up for the inconvenience to Dr. Augustus."

Caesar blinked, "Wow! Johanna, I appreciate them doing that."   He adjusted the knob on the radio. As she took the exit for the airport, he seemed to be trying to find the right words, "Johanna, I understand that you have to work so much. Your sister is doing the best she can to take care of you. Your parents are on SSI, so it's hard."

Johanna nodded her head, keeping her eyes carefully on the road. A Toyota swerved into her lane and she slammed on brakes and honked.   The car braked and slowed.

Caesar twisted in his seat to look at them as they passed. "They're trying to read the signs."   He looked at Johanna, then went back to the radio, punching buttons mindlessly. After the last one, he went on carefully, "My parents take care of me. I stay in the dorms on campus and they send me money every month."   He shook his long, black, silky hair. "They 100% pay for my education."

"Must be nice."   She was trying to see past the blind spot.

"I don't have any bills, just wants."   She glanced at him quickly. He smiled back at her, the cute smile that showed the chip in his front tooth.   "I am spoiled, but I am working on that really hard. I mean, I've got that job now. It will give me some experience."

Johanna gripped the steering wheel tightly and decided to stay in her lane, "I'm going to college to get a better paying job that will help provide better for me and Lydia."

He rubbed his J. Crew jeans. "Johanna, I want to ask you a question?"

"What, Caesar?"

"What do you think of Mr. Jeremiah?"

She was trying to read the signs, looking for the ones that said Arrival and Departure. "Why do you ask, Caesar?"

"When you and he were at the restaurant I could tell he was coming on strong to you and he is twice your age."

She pulled into the lane for departures and had to slam on brakes too quickly, "Caesar, I am a grown woman; I can handle it."

"Yes, you remember you said that with your last one," his voice was hard, "and he mistreated you." Caesar studied the dashboard, "Johanna, you told me that Mr. Paul is paying you to host Mr. Jeremiah."

"Yes," Johanna answered. "Caesar, it's a lot of money. We need this. We're short on the rent."

He sunk low in the seat and muttered, "Johanna, this man wants you for more than a tour guide." He crossed his arms, "Johanna, we have been friends too long and I am saying this to you because I care for you."

She pulled up at the curb and stopped, hard, "Caesar, here we are at the airport now. I will see you later at the open house."

Caesar leaned over and hugged her, although she was stiff. He got out of the car and pulled his bag from the back seat. The cop waved her to move on. Caesar stood staring as she drove off. Her phone rang. She saw him in the rear view mirror, just standing there, watching her leave, as she fumbled for her phone, "Hey, Sis."

There was no preamble. "What are you going to do about Caesar?"

Johanna gripped the phone. "Listen, I can't talk now. I'm in really bad traffic."

She dropped the phone and moved over one lane.

When she got back to the apartment, she tried to quietly open the door, but Lydia was sitting in the living room with the TV on, pacing back and forth. "We need to talk." She ignored Johanna's groan. "Johanna, I love you but be careful. You have two men competing for you."

Johanna sighed. Was this ever going to end? She tried to think of something to say, then shrugged.

As Johanna moved past, Lydia grabbed her hand, "Johanna, before you go, let's pray."

Johanna couldn't go anywhere with that death grip on her fingers, "Ok."

Lydia pulled her down to the couch, and shifted forward. She closed her eyes, then opened them, reached forward and gripped both of Johanna's hands, then closed her eyes again. "Lord God, cover my little sister. Bless her as she is in the air and in Stone Mountain. Lord, keep her life and raise her up to be that Proverbs 31 women you spoke of in your word." Johanna realized she was staring and hastily shut her eyes, "Bless Caesar and his family as well. In Jesus name we pray."

Johanna blinked a few times. Wow, she felt …. Hmm. Different somehow. "Thanks, Lydia, I needed that prayer."

Lydia hugged her and brushed her hair slightly.

Johanna saw the clock, "Well, let me pack my suitcase because Mr. Paul's driver will be here in an hour to take me to his company plane."

Johanna went in her bedroom and put on her sun dress and red heels. And, of course, a little makeup to bring out her hazel eyes. She was just about ready when there was a knock at the door.

"It's Mr. Paul's driver." Lydia yelled. Johanna came out, trying to wheel the suitcase, but it stuck on the carpet. Lydia came from holding the door and tugged it, then helped her sister with the suitcase. She hugged Johanna and stood at the door watching as the driver opened the Bentley's door. Johanna waved to her from the car, then slid in. She waved again, but Lydia couldn't see through the tinted glass. As the car moved out, Johanna watched her sister's lips, "Lord God, please work this out for Johanna."

The trip to the airport was a lot smoother than the one Johanna took earlier. The driver took her to what seemed like a line of private jets, then stopped the car. Johanna shivered and smiled as she looked up at the sleek silver plane, parked at an angle. The driver opened her door, and she stepped out of the spacious auto. The driver gently closed the door and followed her across the tarmac, carrying her suitcase. She bit her lip to keep her grin from getting too big as she moved past two pilots by the wheels doing maintenance checks. She nodded to their greeting, then started up the stairs, past the uniformed steward, and into the open door of the private jet.

...

Johanna came up the escalator at the Atlanta Airport, merged into the milieu and walked slowly through the throng to the left. On her side were all the travelers. On the other side of the divide was a searching throng, the farthest anyone was allowed without passing through Security. She peered past a mother with two small boys carrying balloons and a sign that read "Welcome Home!" She studied the placards, but the names were wrong: "Smith," "Davis," "Jackson." Where was Caesar?

"Johanna!"

Behind the balloons, she spotted Caesar, pushing through the crowd, waving, followed by a tall man. With a final push, they were together. He enveloped her in a hug, then kissed both cheeks with a flourish.

"Hi, Caesar, and you must be Dr. Augustus!"

"Yes, I am. Johanna, I have heard so much about you from

my brother. Wow! You are prettier than I thought."
"Thanks," Johanna smiled between the two.

After they left the airport and drove to his house in Stone
Mountain, Johanna gulped, "Wow, sir, you have a beautiful
home."

He eased into the driveway, "Thank you."

She was staring out the window at the big rock that seemed
to stick out of nowhere, its grayness merging with the blue
sky. "It's beautiful up here."

He cut the engine, "Thank you! Well, come on in." He
pulled open the trunk and easily lifted out her suitcase. She
followed him into the grand foyer, and looked around at the
soft blues and the open spaces.

He set her suitcase down, "Welcome!" He waved an arm,
"Would you like something to drink?" She shook her head,
"Caesar?"

Caesar was intent on Johanna. She couldn't think of
anything to say.

Dr. Augustus looked at both of them, "OK! Well, let me
show you to your room." He led them up a spiral staircase
and turned right down a hall, "You will have your own
bedroom and bath." He pushed open a door and gestured
for her to go first. She stepped into a lavish room with a
canopied bed. "Caesar and I will be on the other side." He
stepped over to the window. The drapes opened with a
flourish revealing a backyard with tall trees surrounding a
deck with a pool. In the background was the mountain, tall
and proud.

"Is there anything you need?" She shook her head and he went on, "The open house will start in two hours. Johanna, this is a big day for me. It's our second facility. At this clinic we will do more outpatient surgeries."

She looked up at his enthusiasm, "Well, Dr. Augustus, I can't wait to see it."

He was at the door, surveying the room one last time, "Oh yes, Johanna, the rest of the family will be here from Rome in a few minutes, so come downstairs once you get relaxed."

Well! Johanna kicked off her shoes and dug her toes in the thick Persian rug. She dumped her purse on the bed and moved across the carpet onto the smooth wooden floors and then to the gray slate in the bathroom. The sunken tub looked SO inviting, but there just wasn't time. There was a full length pencil sketch of a nude woman looking at water. She couldn't make out the artist.

She moved back to the bedroom and studied some modern art on the wall, then rubbed her hand across the silk duvet. She plumped the pillows and studied a painting. She tried to think back to Art Appreciation, but she'd forgotten Rothko.

She wandered back into the bathroom, turned a tap on, and pulled out a drawer. She stroked her hand over the towel set, found a blow dryer and an iron. That would come in handy.

She wandered over to the sketch again, looking at it closely. It was a woman, but Johanna looked closer. The woman and her reflection in the water didn't seem to match. Johanna stared at the picture, mesmerized. The image in the water was very unlike the nude woman, tranquilly looking down. Her reflection looked, what? Vibrant, that's what it was. Johanna glanced back and forth from the woman to her reflection. The woman looked elegant, demure, unavailable, and disinterested with her head turned away. But in the water, her reflection changed. Johanna studied the image, trying to identify the change. She looked like someone who was very aware of her body. Her reflection wasn't demure and disinterested. In the reflection, every cell pulsated with life. Johanna swallowed. In the reflection, just a few pencil strokes made the woman look really, really sexy.

She just had to call Lydia, "Wow, girl, you would not believe it! Caesar's brother's got it going on. His house is huge. He's got a pool and a Jacuzzi. My bathroom, just my bathroom, has two sinks, a tub, a shower, a closet, and it's as big as your bedroom!"

An hour later, she held the gleaming bannister down the spiral staircase feeling ready for anything. Through the bay windows, she saw a Mercedes in the circular driveway. It looked like the family was arriving. There was a crowd in the foyer, spilling into the living room, laughing and hugging each other. As she reached the bottom, Dr. Augustus looked up from his bear hug on an elderly woman. "Here she is! Johanna, come meet everyone!"

After the hugs and greetings, one older woman turned to her and raised an eyebrow. There was an awkward pause, then she smiled and reached out to take both of Johanna's hands. "Well, Caesar, you did not tell us about your friend."

"Yes, this is Johanna, my best friend from college."

"Johanna, it's a pleasure to meet you. I hope you had a nice flight?" After the polite replies, she turned, "Dr. Augustus, are you ready?"

At the clinic, the press was there to interview Dr. Augustus about his second facility. There was a huge picture of his first location in Atlanta inside the foyer of the new, second, clinic in Stone Mountain. There was a beautiful red ribbon on the door.

Johanna sipped punch politely as Dr. Augustus made a speech. Then it was ribbon time. She applauded politely and was about to follow everyone inside, when a last car pulled up.

The clinic director, standing at the door and welcoming the last of the guests, gasped, then turned abruptly and pushed her way into the room. Johanna was trying to figure out what was going on when Caesar took her by the hand. "Can we talk privately?"

"Yes, of course," Johanna answered.

He pulled her over to a side, then stopped. Caesar couldn't look her in the eye, "Johanna, we have been friends for a long time." His voice was stilted. He must have rehearsed his speech, "I would like to ask you a question." He stopped and seemed to lose his place.

She shifted to her other foot. "Yes?"

"Well, it's like this." A car door slammed behind them.

He stopped and looked past her, "What is he doing here?"

She swiveled her head, "Who, Caesar?"

The clinic director slammed open the door, pulling Dr. Augustus by the hand, excitedly whispering, "I told you it was him."

Johanna stared, baffled, between Caesar's scowl and the hurrying figures of the clinic director and Dr. Augustus. She finally turned completely around, and put up her hand to shield her eyes from the glare.

'The Jeremiah' was standing at the back.

Chapter 6: Stone Mountain

Dr. Augustus hurried up to him, "Mr. Jeremiah! Welcome! Welcome! What brings you to our open house?"

They shook hands, "Well, I asked Mr. Paul what open house it was that my host was going to?" Dr. Augustus clapped him on the back as Jeremiah continued, "My administrator researched it and we found out you are the best neurosurgeon in the country. You have saved a lot of lives."

"I'm so honored you came here. I can't believe you came just for our ribbon cutting."

After a long moment, Jeremiah nodded, "Dr. Augustus, when you get some time, let's talk about offering your services at my company?"

Dr. Augustus rocked back and forth on his heels. He glanced back at the clinic director, "Yes! Of course!" He took a deep breath and seemed to calm down, "Jeremiah, that would be an honor."

Jeremiah looked past him, "Hello, Johanna, you must finish your job hosting me."

Johanna stared between Jeremiah and the car, aware of Caesar's folded arms beside her, as Jeremiah went on, "So I spoke at the convention earlier and took care of my business. Here I am." He looked around and studied the talk granite rock. "This is my first time at Stone Mountain. I hope we can see some sites while I am here."

A bird swooped overhead. The driver gently shut the car door. When Johanna continued to gape, Jeremiah went on, "Johanna, my time is limited. I really enjoy your company so please don't be mad at me for surprising you." She was vaguely aware that she ought to do something, say something. Jeremiah turned to Dr. Augustus, "I hope you don't mind my coming out."

Dr. Augustus looked at his brother's hand on Johanna. He started to speak, then stopped himself. After a long, long moment, he muttered, "Not at all." He hesitated, then shrugged, not glancing at Caesar, "Why don't you come on in and join us?"

When Jeremiah walked through the door, the noise level stayed the same. But after a few moments, it got quieter and quieter. Johanna, furtively standing at the door, began to hear the whispers. "Isn't that Jeremiah? The one on TV?"

The whispers grew louder, "I can't believe he is here." Jeremiah stayed and talked with the family. At the earliest time he politely could, he asked if they minded if he took Johanna away for the evening.

All eyes swiveled to her. A few turned to look at Caesar, and their eyes shifted between the two.

Jeremiah asked, "Johanna?"

She hated being the center of this attention, "Just a minute."

The conversation started again, lower this time, as Johanna pulled Caesar to a corner. She leaned in against the noise, "What did you want to say?"

He shook his head, "Nothing. Go ahead and have fun."

"No earlier; you wanted to say something."

"It wasn't important. This isn't a good time."

She looked around the party, "Ok, but let's talk later, Caesar."

"Sure," he nodded, picking up a drink from a passing waiter.

Well, outside Mr. Paul had made arrangements with a luxury car company in Stone Mountain to pick up Johanna and Jeremiah and take them around. Of course, the family saw the limo when it pulled up.

Caesar came outside and stood on the steps, watching Johanna laugh as she stepped into the limo. His uncle came up beside him, "That girl doesn't know you like her."

Caesar scowled but said nothing. His aunt came up and pulled on his uncle's arm. As he turned to go back inside, his uncle looked back one more time, "If you don't say something, you will lose Johanna."

Caesar got another drink and went to the side of the house, where the guys were hanging.

Well, Johanna got into the limo and settled herself comfortably on the nice leather. The driver looked into the rear view mirror, "Mr. Jeremiah, where are we going?"

"We have reservations at Stone Mountain at the Terrace for dinner and a laser show."

Johanna squealed, "Jeremiah! You are wonderful!"

Once they pulled up at the mountain, people were staring at the limo, waiting to see who would emerge. Johanna got out next to Jeremiah. People started trying to get his picture as he smiled and waved at the crowd.

She looked around, and he put his hand on the small of her back and directed her forward.

"Mr. Jeremiah and Miss Johanna, we're so glad you could join us." Johanna wondered how this distinguished gentleman knew them. "I'm the director of the park."

Oh.

Jeremiah's hand snaked into hers.

"This way, please."

Jeremiah released her hand, gestured for Johanna to go first, and she followed the director up some stairs to a corner table on the terrace. What a terrific view to watch the show! "This is great, I am not used to this."

Jeremiah smiled and sat down. "Perfect!"

The director smiled, "We're so glad you could see the show. We hope you enjoy it."

Jeremiah nodded as the director smiled, waved to a waiter to come over, and left.

Jeremiah turned to Johanna, "Stick with me! You haven't seen the rest of what I will do for you." He leaned forward, gazing into her hazel eyes, "Johanna, I am so impressed with you. This is a little soon, I was planning to tell you later, but I've been thinking. I would love to give you a job in my company. Also relocate you and Lydia to Texas."

Johanna choked, then coughed. "But what about Lydia's job?"

Jeremiah waved his hand, "My company always has room for a legal secretary." He pressed on, "I will cover all your expenses and take care of your education." He sat back. A waiter came up and began pouring water, "You don't have to answer today, just think about it." He looked at the mountain, then back at her thoughtfully, "I know, why don't you pray about it?"

She tried to think of something to say, "Why me?"

He smiled gently, "I love your style and your ambition to have a career to support your family. Lydia needs a break in her career and in her life. I have studied you, Johanna. You are a good woman that needs a break and if you will, allow me to give you a start?"

Jeremiah reached over and used his thumb to wipe a tear falling from her eyes.

"Thank you, Jeremiah, for finding favor in me."

He laughed, then nodded at the waiter. "I hope you like barbeque because we Texans love it." She laughed through her tears and he sat back, "I already ordered our meals."

As they ate, they were facing the mountain and lake that ran right in front. A waterfall sparkled in the lighting. She took a final bite and sat back, "Jeremiah, you are a beautiful man inside and out."

He hesitated, "Johanna, I was not sure of the age difference."

She shook her head, "Really, what does age matter?"

He seemed to come to a decision, "I must be honest with you, Johanna. I've got some personal business to work out."

Her heart sank, "Don't tell me. You're married."

"My wife and I have been separated for over a year and the paper work is filed in court. Johanna, I will be happy to show it to you." She couldn't look at him, so he kept on. "Right now the holdup is money. She wants half my company. I will not give it to her." He looked up, then back down, "So....will you walk away from me because of this?"

She put down her napkin, "No, Jeremiah, thank you for being honest." She toyed with her glass. "As long as we're being honest, I guess I should tell you."

His face became grim, "It's that boy, isn't it?"

"I do have feelings for Caesar."

His eyes flashed, "Johanna, I can tell he likes you too. So what are your thoughts on me?"

The candle flickered across her face as she touched his hand, "Right now, I am getting to know Jeremiah."

He lifted an eyebrow, "What about Caesar?"

She pulled her hand back, "I coulda been settled on Caesar. But then, you walked into my life, so I am torn between you two. I have not told Caesar how I feel, so he does not know, and I am glad."

"Why?"

"Well," she was looking at her empty stemware, "Now I see something else I might want to pursue."

Jeremiah smiled as the waiter refilled her glass.

The sun was going down as they ate, laughed and talked. Then came the laser show with fireworks. In the middle of the fireworks, Jeremiah leaned across the table and kissed Johanna gently. The sounds of the fireworks diminished in her mind as he turned her face to him and pulled her close. Johanna caught her breath. "Wow, Jeremiah, you are a good kisser."

"Johanna, I know you come from a Christian home. I want to do right by you and God. So that's why I wanted to get that off my chest."

Behind them, there was a slow whistle, then another burst of light. Amid the applause, and the oohs and ahhs, they turned back to the show.

After the laser show, Johanna glanced at her cell phone. "Oh no!"

He stood and held out a hand, "Missed a phone call?"

She took his hand and moved through the crowd. They came to the stairs, "It's not that. I didn't realize the time."

He stopped mid-stair, "You don't have to go to work tomorrow."

"It's just that I'm a guest in Dr. Augustus' home. I don't want to impose by staying out too late."

Jeremiah checked his Rolex. "I will have the driver take you back now, if you like." They came to the entrance; he looked around and waved.

As the limo pulled up, Jeremiah gripped her hand, "Johanna, will you let me know what you decide." The driver came around, "Whatever the choice." The driver held open the door, but Jeremiah's gripped her fingers, "Please don't keep me hanging on."

He released her hand. She flexed her aching fingers and slid into the limo, "I won't."

In the strained silence in the limo, Johanna remembered her manners, "Jeremiah, thank you for a wonderful date; it was magical."
The ride was so smooth past the lines of people trying to exit. Soft music came on the stereo and Jeremiah leaned back. He stroked her arm, then touched her hand, and gripped it, "May I kiss you before you get out of the limo?"

Johanna squeezed his fingers, "Yes."

He gently moved to her, hesitated as the limo went over a bump, and then grazed her lips. He put his hand behind her head and moved in more urgently. The music swelled.

After a time, she realized that the car had stopped. Jeremiah glanced at the door to Dr. Augustus' house, then released his touch on her face, and straightened up. "I am staying at the Westin Hotel in downtown Atlanta. Call me in the morning. I will have the driver take us back to the airport."

"Thank you again for everything."

He was formal now, following her to the door. "The pleasure is all mine." He glanced at the house, pressed her hand, kissed her cheek discreetly, and returned to the car.

She watched it leave, then turned to the door. That was odd. It wasn't shut. It was cracked, just a little bit.

She pushed it open, stuck her head in and looked around, then stepped inside. Her feet tapped loudly on the hardwood floors. She pulled off her shoes and started through the house, then started. Caesar was standing by the baby grand looking out the window. "Oh, it's you! Hi Caesar, I'm surprised you're still up."

He turned from the window, "Just waiting for you, Johanna."

"Why?"

"Johanna, I need to talk to you."

She looked around. The house seemed quiet and dark. "Ok, maybe we should sit out by the pool?"

"Good idea. It's a beautiful night." He opened the patio door, flipped a switch and the pool lights flooded the darkness. "Give me a minute and I will get us some sodas."

She walked out on the deck, breathing the scent of honeysuckle. The cicadas were so loud. An owl hooted. A slight breeze was blowing. The water was blue and inviting from the lights in the pool. The moon was out, and a million stars were shining. She came to a chaise lounge as he slid the patio door shut behind him, "Are these seats all right?"

She sat down, stretched her feet out, and took the can he offered. She popped the lid as he shoved a pool chair next to her.

Johanna took a sip, as a small fountain began burbling on the far end of the pool. She looked at Caesar, then looked away, a knot forming in her belly.

"Johanna, you have been my best friend for years ever since I came to the US." Uh oh. When he talked like this, it was serious. "You and Lydia were my first friends that showed so much love." She put the cold can to her forehead, bit her lip, and nodded to encourage him. "But things have changed."

Where could this be going? "Oh?"

He seemed to be trying to remember a speech. "There is one who I love so dearly."

Her stomach lurched. He wanted to talk about this now? And who was this girl? Johanna thought she knew all his friends. "Who, Caesar?"

"You, Johanna. I am in love with you."

She almost dropped the can. "Oh."

He looked at her determinedly, "Johanna, please let me get this out." She gulped, put the can down carefully, and nodded, "Johanna, if I don't tell you I will lose you to Jeremiah. Before he came, it was you and me. We did everything together and overnight that has changed. You have met this man twice and are hosting him for a weekend." He kicked the plastic leg of the chair moodily, "I see you glowing when he is around." He looked around at the cabana, the dying embers in the fire pit, and the shadowy shape of the rose trestle. "Johanna, that man is rich. I don't have anything like that right now, but once I finish college and start my career, things will be different." She opened her mouth to speak, but he held up his hand, "Johanna, even when I finish college, I may not have money like that, but I will have money to provide for us and then some."

He looked at her cleavage, then his eyes trailed to her legs and down to her freshly manicured feet in their high-heeled, strapped sandals, "Johanna, I have never been with a girl your size and I was wrong for letting that get in my way. Your sister prayed with me on that issue and God has changed my mind. You probably did not even know that your sister prayed for me?"

She closed her mouth and shook her head, "No, Caesar, that is so touching. I have never had a guy pray about us."

He chuckled, "Your sister Lydia is one praying woman."

She smiled in the dark, "That's for sure."

71

"Johanna, I don't want to be your friend anymore." He looked at her with determination, "I want to be your boyfriend! Girl, I want you to be the lady in my life."

Why didn't he say this earlier, like last month? "Oh Caesar, can I say something?"

"Yes, Johanna." He was looking straight at her.

She struggled to think. Her sister's stern face stayed in her mind. Yes, she'd be honest. It was time to lay her cards on the table. But, she bit her lip. How to say this? "I do have feelings for you but Jeremiah asked me tonight to relocate to Texas and bring my sister." She continued with a rush before she lost her nerve, "He will give my sister and me both a job, plus he offered to pay for my education." The breeze swept his dark hair across his burning eyes. She ran out of steam, "I have not even told Lydia yet. You are the first."
Caesar sat back, his abs rippling even as he slumped over. "Wow."

Johanna nodded, pulling her gaze from his bulging shoulders. "Right now I am confused on what to do."

"Johanna, please don't make a quick decision. Think about it. Pray about it."

What could he be thinking? She searched for words, "Caesar you know I have always had low self-esteem and a weakness for the bad boys. But you are different for me. You're a great Catholic and a family guy. Caesar, I love that about you. You have always watched out for me."

A light came on in the house. A TV turned on. Someone

couldn't sleep. "You never put me down even when you met the guys that I dated and you knew they were jerks." He shrugged, turning his face away. "Caesar, you have been that shoulder to cry on every time I got hurt. You have held my hand through college, especially when you knew math was kicking my tail." She leaned forward, but he didn't seem to notice her cleavage. Someone started arguing inside, but the words were too faint to hear. "Caesar, even though you had a problem with my weight, you never showed it. I truly appreciate you for being that great man in my life."

Caesar got up from the chair and paced in front of the pool. He walked over to her, got on his knees, and fell forward in her lap, pulling her to him. Was he crying? He couldn't be, "I shoulda told you. I shoulda. I love you, girl."

Johanna put her hands on her face. She bent forward, his hair was soft when her face touched his.

That was what did it. She really, really didn't mean to say it, she never, ever should have said it, but it just came out. In a voice almost too low to hear, "I love you, too."

He lifted his head up and looked at her. She stroked the hair out of his face, put an arm around his neck, and traced his cheeks with her finger. She kissed the top of his cheekbone gently, "Caesar, you are my sunshine. You are my light that I see when my day gets tough."

She brushed the side of his face, tracing the places where her tears fell, "Please know Caesar that I will always love you."

Caesar put his hands to her face and breathed deeply. He

put his forehead to hers, then pulled her close and kissed her deeply. He pulled away, cupping her face.

"You owe me a date, Johanna."

What was this? "Ok."

He took her hand. "What about a late night swim?"

She looked around at the clear, blue water. "Sure."

The pool was great. Johanna rode on Caesar's back and he liked having those chocolate legs all around him. He ducked, and came up the other side. She swam away, then turned, and tossed him a ball, smiling radiantly. He batted it back.

She ducked, "Caesar, this is a side of you I did not know you had. I like to see you have fun. I hope to see this side of you some more."

He dove under the water, his hair trailing.

The next morning, she had to call Lydia.

It took some time to explain exactly what was happening with Jeremiah and Caesar. "Yes, that's right. Jeremiah wants to relocate us, yes, both of us, really. To Texas. I know. I know. Yes, both of us. He's offered us great jobs, a place to live, and on top of that, the company will pay for college. Really. No, I didn't say anything."

Johanna stretched out on the Egyptian cotton sheets and stroked the duvet, then rolled onto her stomach, the sun streaming warm. With the bathroom door open, she could see the picture, the woman still staring at the water, her reflection so different, so alive. "Yes, that's right. Caesar! It was just maybe an hour or so later. I know. No. Honestly, I didn't do anything to encourage him talking. I couldn't believe it either. Well, how was I to know how Caesar felt? He never said a word." She sat up and plumped the pillows behind her, "Sis! What am I going to do?"

She nodded a few times.

"I agree, but we graduate pretty soon." She shook her head, exasperated, "I am not too young."

Her sister's voice was clear, "Johanna, you know Mom always told us to seek God in everything we do. Then you know Dad always told us to keep our word."

Johanna agreed, but she couldn't figure out how that applied, "I know, I know. But what about this situation? What about now?"

Her sister's voice was thoughtful, "Sis, you've got to make a big decision."

There was a knock on the door. Johanna interrupted, "Hold on, sis."

It was Caesar, reminding her of their date. She just had half an hour; she'd have to cut this talk short.

"Ok, Lydia. I'm back."

Lydia must have been thinking, "Johanna, let's do this. I get vacation coming up and you will be finished with summer school in a little bit. Let's take a trip to Texas and see what Jeremiah's company has to offer and check out the colleges?" Hmm, what a good idea. "Don't make a decision. Explore your options and go to God with everything. Tell Caesar and Jeremiah you need to check things out and see what all is out there. But whatever you do, don't commit to either one until you explore all your options." Almost as an afterthought, her sister continued, "Don't drag them along either. Be a lady in this matter."

"Yes, Ma'am."

"Love you, sis.

"You too."
"Keep me posted."

"I will."

That was reasonable. She'd be logical. She'd do the intelligent thing. She'd think it over and make the decision that made sense. Her heart trembled within her and she looked in the mirror. The nude woman in the bathroom showed in the mirror right beside her head. She studied the woman and her vibrant reflection for a very long time. Both were so very different.

Chapter 7: Caesar's Move

She'd always been fast in the mornings, so she was ready in record time. Caesar took her to a restaurant called Kitty's which had a great breakfast buffet. It had an old country western look and was right by the lake. They took their plates outside on the patio, and sat with the warm sunshine on their faces.

Caesar finished his coffee and looked around, "I had a nice time at the pool."

Johanna speared a strawberry, "Me, too."

He sat next to her, their thighs touching slightly. "So, how do you feel knowing that I love you?"

"Caesar, I can't believe just how much."

He sat back, turned to her and touched her hair, "Johanna, I coulda told you. I have been holding this back for too long."

Johanna thought for a moment, "I am no better. I let your race get the best of me. But I realize that was wrong of me. Color does not mean a thing. God is not pleased with vanity." She put her fork down, then twined her fingers in his.

"Johanna, I brought you gift." He reached into his pocket and pulled out a box.

She gasped, then opened it to see a necklace with a diamond on it. "Oh Caesar, that's so pretty."

"It belonged to my late aunt and she gave it to me before she passed. I was always her baby nephew." He smiled, remembering, "She wanted me to have something to remember her by."

She started shaking her head and pushed the box towards him, "I can't take this."

He folded her hands over the box, "I want you to have this. I want you to have something that shows I love you." She was stumped, "Will you wear it?"

She swiped her cheek, then turned sideways in the booth so he could put it on her.

He fumbled with the clasp and then smoothed the chain. "Johanna, I care for you and I just want you happy."

Her hand wouldn't stray from the diamond, "Caesar, I've got a lot of thinking to do."

The waiter came up. "More coffee?" Caesar looked at her. They both shook their heads.

"Well, I've got one more thing for us to do. Let's finish this breakfast and we've got a boat to catch."

She sat back, "What?"

"Yes, a boat ride on the lake."

....

Johanna leaned back in her seat, watching Caesar warily. She didn't think he'd ever piloted a boat before, but men and their toys.   She opened her mouth to ask, then hesitated.   Maybe it was better not to know.

This lake was stunning.   The mountain loomed overhead, casting a stunning reflection on the clear water.   She lifted her face to the sunshine, and studied the clouds overhead. A bird (or was that a hawk?) swooped from a tall pine, glided over the lake, and then pumped its wings to turn. The bird then rose past the trees to soar in lazy circles, high overhead.   Another floated high in the distance.   Her neck was starting to hurt, so she came back to Caesar.   His hair was blowing behind him as he gripped the steering wheel (was that what you called it on a boat?).   The boat swerved, raising a wake right beside her.   She wanted to trail her hand in the water, but the large boat was too high.   The boat swerved towards the other side as Caesar pushed down the throttle.   He glanced at her, grinning.   She gripped the seat and smiled nervously.

"How did you get this boat again?"

"What?"

"The boat."

He shook his head at her.   She waved her hand around as the boat zoomed past a fishing boat, leaving a rolling wake.

He powered the boat down, "What were you saying?"

The quiet was deafening.   "How did you get the boat?"

"Augustus upgraded last year," He shrugged, trying to act nonchalant, then slowly increased the speed.   He looked at her, then steered the boat towards the shore.   The wind whipped her face. There were so many flowering bushes around here. He guided the boat slowly near a cove, then powered it down. "Want something to drink?" He didn't wait for answer, but went into the small galley and rummaged around, then came back up and handed her a bottle.

It was starting to get a little warm. "Come on over here." The boat rocked a bit as she moved next to him. What a great view of the mountain. She relaxed on the cushions, waves lapping the side of the boat, the smell of the water clean and crisp, mingling with the pines that shot up all around the lake. She followed the image of the boat in the water, then wondered if she really looked like that girl she saw, the one who was her reflection. After a moment, he put an arm around her and pulled her closer.

She looked up and smiled. The wind was whipping his long black hair, and she stroked it from his face. "You had a full date for us!"

"Yes, Johanna, and brother was a big help, too."

"Well, I intended for us to play golf over on the other side of the lake as well." She sat up and shaded her eyes. So that's what all that green space was.

He pulled her back, "As you can see, the course is beautiful and it has a scenic view of the mountain. But I know you have to catch the plane back to Philly."

There didn't seem to be another boat anywhere around. And the lake was so big! A plane flew overhead, far in the distance. Birds were singing in the trees. "Yes, Jeremiah's got to finish up some meeting with Mr. Paul."

Caesar drank deeply, "I understand." He looked around, opened his mouth, shut it, and then tried again. "Johanna, I shoulda said how I felt sooner but," he winced and mumbled, "I let your weight hold me back." His lips tightened and he looked up, "Now that Jeremiah is in the picture, I know you are torn." He waited, then turned and looked her straight in the face, "Just be honest with me."

"Yes, Caesar."

He took another swallow, "Can I ask you what it is about that man that you like?"

Her face was red again. She never blushed! Well, she never did until Jeremiah turned up. What was going on? "Caesar, can we talk about Jeremiah another time?"

His European manners kicked in, "Yes! We are on a date. This is not the place; besides, let's enjoy the time we have together." Caesar leaned over and kissed her gently. He kissed her another time, searched her face, then hugged her to him. "Johanna, just being in your arms is like watching the sun rise across the lake."

His t-shirt was soft against her face as she listened to his heart thumping. "Caesar, like I said before, you are my knight in shining armor. Truly, you have been there for me." The sun was so warm on the side of her face. A breeze swept over her.

He turned towards her and put both arms around her. She snuggled even closer into him. The hawk called, and its mate answered.

Caesar sat up, "Johanna, please remember me?"

She pulled him back down, "I will always remember you."
…

Back at Dr. Augustus' house, Johanna waved to Dr. Augustus, then looked at her watch, and went upstairs to pack. Caesar sat down next to Augustus to bend his brother's ear about Johanna. "Augustus, she is torn between me and Jeremiah."

His brother opened the refrigerator in the kitchen, "I'm not surprised."

"Why not?"

"Caesar, she is a young college girl. From what you tell me, her family does not have much." Augustus could feel Caesar's bafflement. "You're what? Senior year, right?" He tossed a bottle to Caesar, who caught it mid-air. Augustus shook his head, then clapped his hand on Caesar's should, "Caesar, man, don't put pressure on Johanna. It never works."

"So what then?"

"Are you sure about her? You're still in college."

He waited, but the silence got to him. He relented after studying Caesar's thunderous face. "Get your Bible out and pray."

Upstairs, Johanna was in the huge bathroom, shoving her lipsticks into a makeup bag. She zipped the bag, then turned the silver handle to get a little water to rinse the sink and smiled at her reflection in the huge mirror, framed by lights that covered the wall. She smiled at the nude. She was starting to feel really close to the girl in the pencil drawing, even though she still hadn't figured out the artist. But, it probably didn't matter at this point.

With a final look around, she pulled out her cell phone and called Jeremiah. "I'm ready. Can you send the car for me?"

"Ok, Johanna. See you shortly, my lady."

After Johanna hung up, she started out the door, but then stopped and returned to the picture.   Lightly, not quite touching the image, she traced the lines of the enigmatic form, studying the face that she couldn't quite see.   Her eyes roamed from the standing figure to the reflection in the water, the one that was a little fuzzy, but somehow seemed clearer, curvier, and more alive. Her fingers trailed near the curves on the thighs.   She blinked away a tear. Then another.   The woman, mysterious, unavailable continued to look away.   Her reflection begged for life. Johanna tilted her head slightly, confused again by the picture.   If she looked at the reflection sideways, she couldn't tell which was the real woman.

Johanna fell down on her knees, "Lord God, I don't know what to do. I am so confused. Both of these men are good to me.   God, I love them both. How can that be?"   She squared her shoulders, it was no time to lie to herself, "But I can only chose one."

She rocked back and forth.   She swallowed and swiped her face, streaking mascara on the back of her hand.   She thought back to her mother, stroking her face when she was little.   She gasped a choked breath, remembering the Bible verse they said together every night when she went to bed, the one it took so long to learn, "Even lions go hungry for lack of food, but those who obey the LORD lack nothing good." She stared, unseeing, at the wall, thinking of her mother opening the Bible almost in the middle to Psalms or something like that.

The tears started again, "You know what is best for your child. Please help, God. Lord, I stand on Psalms 34 for I am seeking you. God, show me the right way to go." She looked around the room. Everything looked exactly the same. She started to get up, then remembered, "I pray this in your name. Amen."

She had just enough time to repair the damage to her face before Caesar knocked on the door, "The car is here."

Caesar walked her out to the car and handed the driver her luggage. He stood awkwardly for a moment, then kissed her check. "Bye, Johanna."

She shuffled to her other foot, "Goodbye, Caesar." Then she climbed into the limo beside Jeremiah.

The car pulled out as Jeremiah appraised her, "Hello, Johanna. How are you?"

As she pulled her eyes from the figure at the curb, she could feel the blush starting, "It's good to see you. I'm fine. Great."

He sat back in the seat, "So what do you have planned for us when we get back, Johanna?"

In the side mirror, she caught a last glimpse of Caesar standing and watching, not moving. The car turned a corner, and Caesar vanished from the mirror. The car stopped, then turned again.

After a moment, she remembered the question. She had to think. She leaned forward, and began to grin, her eyes sparkling, "A tour! I've got to give you a tour of downtown Philly."

"Looking forward to it."

...

Sitting in the soft cushion, watching the white clouds go by, laughing and chatting, Johanna didn't see how whatever she offered could possibly compete with the private jet. However, she reminded herself, it wasn't her place to say that.

As the jet landed, Mr. Paul called, "I have the driver waiting on you. He will take you to the horse stables downtown. I have rented a carriage ride for the entire day."

Jeremiah looked over at her then took the jet's phone off speaker. "Thank you, brother."

She busied herself looking out the window, but she could hear pretty well anyway as Mr. Paul went on, "No problem. I want you to have the best." There was a laugh, "Jeremiah, when I come to Texas, you always take care of me."

The Bentley was different but just as luxurious as the private jet. She fingered the soft leather. She could get used to this. Jeremiah kept her fascinated with one story after another when he wasn't staring into her eyes or stroking her hair. He kept pulling his hand back, but it somehow always seemed to be holding her hand or brushing against her. She especially liked the shoulder massage at the end of the plane ride.

The driver took them to the park and dropped them off for the carriage ride.

Johanna had to stop herself from squealing as she climbed up, then settled herself onto the swaying seats, "This is just beautiful. I have never done this before."

Jeremiah sank next to her, then nodded to the driver. The driver tipped his high hat, which matched his long-tailed uniform with the silver buttons, and shook the reins. The horses clomped down the road. The carriage jerked slightly, then smoothly and slowly moved down the road. The sunshine warmed her face as the tourists were gawking and taking pictures.

Jeremiah put an arm around her, "When you are with me, I will treat you like the queen you are."

They passed the restaurant where they first ate, that magical, long-ago evening. Johanna turned her head as they went by, "Jeremiah, have you had something to eat today?"

"Yes, the hotel provided breakfast."

This must have been a long time ago. He picked her up pretty early and then there was the flight when he thanked the steward but said he never ate on planes.

She was trying to add up the hours, when he interrupted, "Johanna, it's time to eat now."

She beamed, back on secure footing, "Ok, Philly has the best cheesesteak sandwiches you'll ever eat." The horse and carriage turned a corner and clomped down the historic section. "Downtown has a restaurant that won the hall of fame for the best cheese steak in the world!"

He laughed, "Ok, Johanna. Let's go!" She tapped the driver and explained. He nodded and turned another corner. An outdoor restaurant was playing jazz. It took a moment for her to catch the song. The same one at the restaurant. She began to hum along. It was the song from Cinderella, "A Dream is a Wish Your Heart Makes."

Johanna looked at her shimmering high-heeled sandals, then traced a finger across her blue gown. Sunlight glimmered on Jeremiah's head, sort of like a crown, as he pointed to a distant tower. She gripped his hand suddenly and he stopped, then smiled at her.
She tried to cover her confusion as the song faded in the background and they moved from the shade of a skyscraper into the sunshine, throngs streaming back and forth. "Once we finish lunch, I am going to take you to Independence National Historical Park."

He leaned forward like he wanted to kiss her, but the carriage jerked. He pulled back, then smiled. She looked around at the watching crowd and babbled, "There is so much to do once we get there."

The carriage pulled up to the cheese steak restaurant. She climbed down, studying her favorite restaurant, then moved forward a bit. He climbed down behind her as a small group of parents and children congregated, staring at the horse. One of the children bravely stepped forward and petted the horse on its side; the animal swished his tail. Jeremiah put his arm on Johanna's back and guided her into the restaurant.

Staring at the billboard, Johanna couldn't decide what to order; then one of the owners leaned forward. "I know who you are."

Heads swiveled and one person in the back stood on tiptoes, peering around, as he went on, "You are the guy that has a world known oil business." He snapped his fingers, "They feature you on CNN and Time. That's who you are."

Jeremiah nodded, "Yes, I am."

"So, what brings you to my place?"

All eyes were staring at them, "My hostess Johanna loves this place. I'm hungry, so here we are."

The owner leaned back and grinned at the people next to him. He stepped forward, "I am honored to have you here. The hoagies are on me today."

Johanna was blushing again. "Thank you so much."

The owner sat them in a private booth with a flourish. "Hope you enjoy lunch."

Jeremiah nodded, then looked down at his hoagie. He

picked it up with both hands, hesitated, and then took an awkward bite. He chewed, then agreed. "This is great!"

The owner walked off with a self-satisfied step.

Jeremiah took another bite, chewed a long time, then took a drink. "Johanna, what do you for fun?"

She closed her eyes, savoring the flavors, then swallowed. She loved, loved, and loved this restaurant. This was Philly! She tried to think: what of all the wonderful things in her city should she talk about? "Here in Philly, we play a game called Halfies."

"Oh? What is that?"

"You don't play it in Texas?"

Jeremiah shook his head, "I've never heard of it."

"Well, we cut a tennis ball in half and hit it with a stick up against a wall." He stopped mid-bite, studying her skeptically. She nodded vigorously, "Jeremiah, when you need a stress reliever, this works! It does for me, anyway." He finished the bite. She breathed deeply, like she always did when she came into this restaurant, then thought some more, "I love to walk in the park and shop." She stopped, "But that's a woman. What about you Jeremiah?"

He seemed to really like Philly cheese steak sandwiches, too. Smart man. "When I am not at my office in Houston, I enjoy the beach. In Texas we call it PINS."

"Jeremiah, what is that?"

"Padre Island National Seashore. It's a great place for swimming and fishing. When you and Lydia come to Texas, I will take you both there." He caught himself. "If you come."

He held the sandwich in his hands, not moving, "Johanna, the oil business can be really stressful. That place is my downtime." He was staring at her now, with that look on his face. "Johanna, as the sun is shining through the window your smile is so radiant!" He looked down at his sandwich, and then put it on the paper plate. "I know I am an older man but you have brought this, hey I might as well say it, this old man so much joy! See, my soon to be ex-wife left little over a year ago for another man." His eyes hooded over, "One of the contractors for my company." He had forgotten the sandwich, "Johanna, you think I am rich. He has double my net worth."

She touched his fingers. After a long moment, they gripped hers. She kept her face calm, but he had a tight hold, "I know that was hard on you."

"Yes, Johanna." He looked around and seemed to come back from his memories, "We have one daughter. She is 18 years old and has a little girl. They are my heart." Johanna didn't know what to say to that, but he kept on as though he wasn't listening, "When she got pregnant, I told her, 'don't abort the baby; let me and your mother help you.' So she did." He shook his head again, his eyes focused, unseeing, on the sandwich. "When her mother left me, she took it so hard. She is the only child and spoiled rotten. Yes, she is daddy's little girl." He released her hand, and she surreptitiously moved it under the table and flexed her fingers. He was concentrating on memories, "In high school she got involved with this basketball guy.

Now, I thought he was a great young man with a full ride scholarship to a division one school but that all changed when he slept with my baby."

He finally picked up the sandwich and took another bite. They ate for a while, and then Johanna decided they might as well get this all out and over with, "What happened?"

He was serious again. She looked out the window at the horse, with more small children around, petting him. Then she looked into the kind eyes in front of her. He shook his head, "Johanna, I believe a man should take care of his responsibilities and I made sure he did that. His parents plus her mother and I got together and worked it out for both of them go to college in Texas. Johanna, they both work part-time and share time with the baby. My daughter decided to live with her mother and not me."

He looked around. "As you see, Johanna, I travel a lot and her mother owns an assisted-living home in Texas. Well, I own 50% of it. I feel her mother can teach her how to be a mother and she needs that. One thing my daughter can say, Johanna, is that I kept her in church. Like your mother, she sings in the choir. Her mother still goes to church but the way she did me, sometimes I wonder."

He looked down at his hands. After a long moment, he unclenched his fists. He took a deep breath, finished his meal and crumbled his napkin. "That's why Johanna I told you if you relocate to Texas, well," he couldn't seem to find the right words, "until I get this divorce worked out." He shook his head and tried to think, "I want to see you but I can't commit until it's right for us. My daughter has got to see one of her parents holding up right living for God."

This was a side to this man she'd not seen, "Jeremiah, you

are so amazing and I love your heart for God."

"Well," he seemed to want to lighten the mood, "Let's go finish this tour."

Chapter 8: Shoulda, Woulda, Coulda?

After they clambered back into the carriage, Jeremiah reached over and gripped Johanna's hand. "Johanna, you may be young but you are so mature for your age."

"Jeremiah, I had to grow up when my parents got sick." A car pulled up next to them, a man lowered his window, leaned out and took a picture of the horse. "Lydia and I have been seeing them every day." He nodded as though he expected that, "Jeremiah, the person who has given the most is Lydia. She put her career plans on hold, downsized her home to help them financially, and she's also helping me with college. Jeremiah, we do what we have to do to survive."

The carriage stopped, "Jeremiah, we are at our first site, the Liberty Bell Center."
He twisted in his seat, "Johanna, the place is so beautiful. I love the design with the brick and glass." They got out and went inside. The lighting in the place really worked; it was easy to read all the old documents. He spent a long time studying the Liberty Bell.

Johanna was perusing a pamphlet. "We can watch a documentary in about ten minutes." She closed the paper. The film might be good, but history was her forte. "A lot of American history took place here in this downtown. Two presidents lived right on High Street: George Washington and John Adams." She kept on. This was one of her passions. "And then, the first African Episcopal Church meeting was held here." He hadn't known that, "James Oronok in 1792."

She went on and on. After a while, his eyes got a glazed look. He waited for her to catch a breath, then took her by the hand and pulled her away from the crowd touring the center. Jeremiah guided her to a corner, looked both ways, then pulled her into a secluded foyer. "Johanna, this has been an amazing weekend for me. I appreciate you being a host for me." He put an arm around her waist and looked into those hazel eyes. "Johanna, I know this was a job and favor to Paul," his eyes roved over her face, "but I hope I will see you after this?"

She couldn't think. She couldn't breathe. "Yes, Jeremiah, I want to get to you know better. If Paul had not have hired me, I would not have met you." She thought hard, then looked up, "The job was a door opener for me." She gripped the hand around her waist and squeezed, "But more than that I have found a new friend that excites me."

"What about your friend, Caesar?"
"Jeremiah, I will tell you what I told him. Please don't ask me. Just let me enjoy you."

"That is fair, Johanna."

She had to get this off her chest, "I will say this, Jeremiah, I have always picked the bad boys in my life but now I am blessed to meet you."

A voice mumbled over the intercom. It wasn't clear, but she'd been here before, "Jeremiah, the movie is about to start."
He started to speak, but the voice on the intercom mumbled again, something about a last call. He put his hand on the small of her back and gestured for her to lead the way. His phone rang.

He hesitated, then pulled it from his waistband and glanced at the number. He frowned. "My daughter." He held up one hand and moved a little ways away from her, then held the phone to his ear.

"Hey baby." He turned around. "What's wrong? Honey, Dinah. I can't hear you. Please stop crying."

Johanna glanced up. He was grim, intent, worried. She could hear Dinah through the phone, "Dad, it's Mom!"

He looked at Johanna briefly, then turned, "What happened, Dinah?"

The words were as loud as if she were on speaker, "Dad, Mom had a heart attack and passed out at work. They rushed her to a hospital in Houston."

In the distance, Johanna could see the lights flashing for the last call for the movie. The cell phone crackled, "Dad, I know you and Mom are going through a divorce, but I'm at the hospital and they won't talk to me. You are still on her medical insurance."

Johanna didn't know what to do. Should she give him some privacy? Stay? The voice on the phone was garbled, then came in clearly, "Daddy, they have her on life support. It doesn't look good. Please, please come home."

"Dinah, wait. Stop. Ok. Tell me again. Who's there with you? What kind of procedures are they doing?"

The voice was garbled again. "She's stable. They're running tests but they won't get the results, all of them, for awhile. They've started, well I forget what, but they'll reevaluate her progress tomorrow. If this doesn't work, they have to operate." He started to speak, but the frantic voice went on, "Her boyfriend is here but he can't sign anything because all her decision making is still in your name."

"OK, Dinah, don't worry. I'm on my way."

"Oh Daddy, thank you." There was a murmur of voices in the background, and then the voice came in again, "You're coming?"

"I'll be there as soon as I can."

"Ok, bye, Daddy."

"I love you. I'll be there soon." He clicked off, then turned to Johanna, "We'll finish the date later, ok?"

"Yes," Johanna couldn't seem to think straight, "I pray she will be ok." He was already guiding her back to the street. He started to speak, but she held up a hand, "Don't worry about me. Just do what you have to do."

He began grimly punching buttons on the cellphone. "Paul? I need to fly out again. Ok. Good."

He strode to the curb, "Taxi!" A cab screeched up. He urgently dismissed the carriage driver, then practically shoved Johanna into the cab and climbed in, "Mr. Paul's office, the Big Towers. Make it quick."

The cab jerked from the curb and she fell against Jeremiah. This wasn't the Bentley. "Johanna, I want you to fly back with me to support me as my friend in case she does not make it."

She shook her head, "I couldn't. This is a family time. Your family."

His phone rang again, he pulled it out, then clicked it off, "Johanna, she still is the mother of my daughter." He grabbed her arm to brace her as the car careened around a corner, "Johanna, if you want Lydia to come that will be fine with me. You two can stay in my guest house." This was happening too fast, "I have a mansion in Spicewood, Texas that sits on 12 acres."

The taxi slammed on brakes amid honking horns. She looked out at the fists shaking and started to answer, then stopped.

At Paul's office, Jeremiah kissed Johanna and then got out of the car. He peeled off some bills and ordered the cab driver to get her home. He leaned in the window, looking twenty years older, lines visible in his grey face. "Call me later, Johanna, and let me know what you decide."

Paul was just getting off the elevator, "I see you and Johanna are getting close." He looked again, "Hey man, you ok?"

He looked from the retreating taxi to Jeremiah, "If I were you, I woulda made her come, I wouldn't let her leave. Why didn't you?"

Jeremiah rubbed his hand through his hair, "Maybe I shoulda." He watched the taxi vanish around a corner. "Paul, it's Ruth. She had a heart attack and Dinah called me. That's why I need the jet. Can I use it to fly back?"

"Sure, Jeremiah, sure. I'm so sorry." It only took a minute

to decide, "Man, Jeremiah, I'm coming with you. Hey, we all went to school together."

....

In the taxi, Johanna called Lydia. It took a while to explain. Lydia just couldn't follow it, but finally Johanna started from the beginning. It was hard to remember all of it, everything about Caesar.

"Yes, I still have the necklace. I mean we've been friends forever. Yes, ok, fine, it's none of your business, but yes, he makes my heart melt. No, I didn't. Well, I shoulda. Do you really think so? Yeah, me too. I admit it. I woulda. I don't know. Yes, you're right. Well, no, I don't know. Maybe I coulda."

This was starting to give her a headache, but that was nothing before they got into Jeremiah. She'd forgotten to mention he was married, sort of. It took a while to get through, "She's his soon-to-be ex."

When she finally got it, Lydia gasped, "Johanna where does that leave you in this picture?"

Johanna bit her lip, "I shoulda gone with him. If it had been any other time. It just wasn't working out. I mean, I woulda, I guess." Her voice was wistful. "Everything happened so fast. I had to make a decision. Do you think it was the wrong one? Do you think I coulda?"

Lydia's voice was low, "Shoulda, woulda, coulda...."

Pam Willis-Hovey is the host of *Unity with Pam Television Show,* a weekly talk-show dedicated to bringing unity between cultures and races.

She is married to the love of her life, retired Sgt. Harry R. Hovey and she is the step-mother of three children and one granddaughter.